Three and me

Abbey Woolgar

Copyright © 2020 Abbey Woolgar
All rights reserved
ISBN: 9798634004983

Dedication

To Zac, Walt and Colin

I love you and am so very proud of all you
Thank you for making my life so full of great tales to tell

To Mum

We all love you very much
Thank you for always being there for us

To Sue

Top Editor
Thank you for taking the time to listen to my terrible tales

To Rufus and Percy

The best cuddling creatures we know
Thank you for putting up with the madness around you

Covid-19

ASD in our house means that self-isolating is fine as long as there are fish fingers. Keeping 2 metres away from other people is also fine and should be adhered to at all times. Quite frankly, if I didn't know where Coronavirus had started from I would say that Zac and Walt summoned up this strange period in the year to make everyone realise how much you can get done, reflect and make sense of things when you slow down. It may also be a way of making the wider public see that sometimes having a social communication disorder can be advantageous.

Both Zac and Walt have been, like the rest of the nation, a little anxious about the whole thing but they have been practicing social distancing for 19 years. They have been a little anxious, like the rest of the nation, about going out with the dogs, which is something they usually really enjoy. We have laid strict rules down and created social stories for what is a really weird time in their lives. We have even talked about death and where we would like to be scattered. Walt's was the best he would like to be cremated with all of his soft toys (he has over 100) and scattered in the sea.

My biggest concern at the moment is that their usual birthday routine, they will be 20 at the end of April, of eating their way round as many restaurants as they can will have to be either put on hold or we will have to come up with a new tradition or we will have to postpone their birthday until later in the year.

Mind you the biggest challenge is still selecting the right gifts. At the grand old age of 19 we are still not sure if they still believe in Santa Claus but Christmas is still an interesting time of year for us. This year Santa got it all wrong. Santa gave the wrong presents, things that weren't even asked for. It is still safe to say that opening presents and showing fake gratitude has not been developed, it is still brutal honesty and opinion all the way.

Zac still likes a 'nice drink' when we are out and about but Walt has now taken this to an adult level and included the consumption of the odd alcoholic beverage mostly fruit based varieties because these are apparently healthy. Our favourite drunken Walt moment was picking him up from a rare social experience where he had partaken of a couple of Ciders. A very giggly Walt got into the back of the car but proceeded to tell his dad to drive slower because everything seemed very fast and blurry, even though we were still stationary.

As we have been told to stay home for at least 4 weeks and only go out once a day this seems a great time to finish writing the third installment of what will now be my trilogy! There are of course other reasons for finishing it. Not just that now I have a captive audience to sell to but that I have been promising all those people who have been part of our lives that they too would get a special mention in my next book. Here it is, let's hope it measures up to the success of my last 2 books and the whopping retirement fund that has built from sales which stands at the grand total of £71.67 to date.

I have continued to deliver presentations on ASD and the tales of Zac and Walt, promoting my books as I go to cover my travel costs. You can see by my massive earnings that I did that well ☺. The best presentation I did was in Bedford some 6 months ago. I had been asked to deliver to a group of nursery teachers as part of a conference. I had been given a slot of 2:45, usually the graveyard shift; people start to think about going home and what they are going to have for tea. I had the whole morning to kill before my turn. Walt was at home so I asked him if he would like to come and support his Mum and show how great he had become. He actually agreed, until I Googled the venue to prepare him for what lay ahead. Once I had also seen the sheer size of the venue and that it held 300 people my nerves genuinely kicked in. Walt declined and I went along with very shaky legs. Luckily when I got there I was greeted by a familiar face and told it was ok there were only about 180 people there today. I was ushered to the back of the auditorium and asked to give my presentation to the media team. At this point I was given a Madonna headset and instructed on the use of the clicker but this was no ordinary clicker as it had all sorts of magical buttons.

The stage was massive and very high so my usual pacing up and down had to be curbed a bit especially because my legs felt like jelly. All in all the presentation went well, I got a couple of questions and a very loud round of applause but I left very quickly, mainly so that I could get ahead of the Bedford school run traffic and process the experience.

Usually after this kind of thing I get a thank you email or a bottle of wine for my trouble but with this one there seemed to be nothing, until about 2 weeks later when this landed in my inbox:

Dear Abbey

I hope you're well. I just wanted to thank you again for your wonderful contribution to our Early Years SEND Conference on 16th October, and share with you some of the comments from delegates on their evaluations.

These comments were in response to the question **'what did you find the most useful part of the day?'**

'I particularly liked the talk from the parent, it was like having a snap shot into family life'
'Abbey Woolgar gave a very inspiring account as a parent with children who have autism'
'Abbey's presentation was such a positive 'good news' story – thanks for sharing'
'Listening to Abbey's experiences'
'Always really powerful to listen to real lives. Abbey was very thought provoking'
'Abbey's strategies for supporting children with autism'
'Fantastic to hear a parent's journey from such a positive disposition. Great message for parents to celebrate their children and celebrate achievements, including small steps. Gave really practical advice and strategies'.
'Listening to Abbey, she was just brilliant. What an inspirational woman!'
'Parent's voice'
'Nice to hear a "parent's voice"'
'I've had a great day! Wanted to hear more from both Dave and Abbey'

I didn't meet Dave but I was pleased that he had done well too. I of course replied saying same time again next year?

Recently I have been delivering more adult based presentations. A somewhat different slant on my usual "this is Zac and Walt from 0-5" session, which of course include the delights of poo. It is hard not to mention poo, picture schedules and forward planning in these more adult sessions because these are still so very key in our lives. Yes things are now easier than they were when the boys were 5 but life still throws the odd curve ball but I hope this never changes because this is the bit that brings us so much fun, laughter and stories for my books

One recent presentation I did in front of some very senior people at work started really well. I had prepared 6 slides, detailed notes and had been briefed that I needed to focus on how ASD affects or should be considered in recruitment, management and career progression. Off I went. I had given myself a good talking to about not talking about poo at any point during this one. I don't think the majority of the audience would have been ready for that. It went very well right up until the moment I went off on a tangent and totally forgot how I was going to relate the story back to one of the 3 things I had been asked to focus on. This was and will be forever known as my first official senior moment. My mind went completely blank and so the third and probably real reason for writing this book is that I figure I really should start to write down the last 7 odd years' worth of stories properly so they don't get lost.

It is safe to say that Zac and Walt have grown into men's bodies but underneath they are still about 10 or so. Routine and planning are still key but this now brings some advantages with it in that I have 2 great house elves who don't deviate from the schedule. Every day the house is hovered and mopped. On Monday night the bins are put out for the bin men and on Tuesday morning they are brought back in. There is always the smell of fish fingers from lunchtime, which they cook, and I can guarantee the dogs will have been fed by 4:15pm everyday. Most parents with young adults without ASD always stand like goldfish when I suggest that this is a benefit of having twins with autism and they ask if I hire them out. Of course I say no but that doesn't mean I don't *think, "Of course, how's £15 per hour?"*

I still refer to them as my children, which causes all sorts of confusion when making telephone bookings because the cashier will always respond "Ok so that's 2 adults and 2 children" and I often find myself having to say sorry no they are nearly 20 now much to their added confusion because really how many 20 year olds still go on holiday or days out with their ageing Mum and Dad! They will always be lovingly known as the boys, fellas, Zed and Dub and occasionally but only when they've been naughty Zachary and Walter.

The somewhat bumpy journey

Secondary school was not as we would have hoped. It didn't start well, it didn't end well and there were some very interesting bits in the middle.

Independently of school Zac and Walt achieved both D of E Bronze and Silver. Both started to learn how to play musical instruments for the skill sections - Zac drums and Walt guitar. Both of them absolutely loved the residential aspects of these. We would drop them off for the expeditions and really looked forward to their stories about the adventures they had. They would always come back smelling interesting but they had a fantastic time. With this in mind, we thought let's combine the music and residential bits and send them on the school music tour to Holland.

They left school on the coach at 5am packed up with media items and enough food to feed a small army. By 9am I had received 10 text messages from them both saying they didn't like it and that the other people on the coach were too noisy. I had of course tried to reassure them that this was probably just excitement and to turn their music up if they were being disturbed.

By lunchtime, they had called me to tell me they didn't like the ferry as there were too many people on it and it smelt funny. This went on pretty much for the whole day until I am guessing they were given melatonin by the teaching staff and they retired to bed.

The next day I text them to tell them they were scheduled to go to Zaanse Schans, billed as: "The Best Place To See Windmills In Holland". I should point out that it is also a place to find locally produced cheese. Zac hates cheese. He hates the smell, the taste and the texture. The other thing to point out is that Zac and Walt really aren't good at exploring places and really need to be fully engaged in an activity in order to get the best out of it. To be fair to Zaanse Schans it was never going to be somewhere that would get the boys excited. Both Zac and Walt called me in tears saying they hated it, it smelt bad, there were too many people and that they wanted to leave. They had been told that they had 3 hours free time to spend there - a nightmare for them but for the other students an absolute dream. Zac's description of the set free time was "we have to do nothing here for hours". While they were on the phone I came up with a quick schedule of events using trusty Google to assist. I text them a plan:

1. Go to the giant clogs and take a picture of each other
2. Count the number of windmills you can see
3. Go to the museum and look around for something interesting to talk to me about
4. Count the mini clogs in the shop
5. Look at the chocolate shop and buy some if it looks nice
6. Go for a walk along the river
PS Zac it will smell of cheese try and avoid it if you can!

Those activities took them all of about 20 minutes so I called the school to ask if they could check in on the boys and ask why they had been left to wander by themselves. The school called the teachers on the trip and this is what they replied:

Dear Mrs Woolgar,

I have spoken to Ms Newton who assured me that she could see both boys and they appeared to be ok. She was going to speak to them after we finished speaking and hopefully make some suggestions.

The boys will not be on their own tomorrow – the plan was always that they stayed in groups with an adult. Both boys are with Ms Newton and they have no free time at all. She will ensure they are ok and confident for the rest of the trip.

Hope this is ok – Sue

They were most certainly not on their own the next day. The teachers on duty took them under their wing and showed them all of the cultural parts of Amsterdam including a cafe with cannabis brownies, a local beer garden and the illusive red windows. We didn't sign the boys up for the music tour the following year.

Cooking at secondary school was a challenge. Our favourite times were when we received these emails:

Dear Mrs Woolgar,

Zac had a cookery assessment today in which he had to follow instructions without assistance. (Due to it being an assessment). He had written a plan that stated that he had to use a frying pan to cook the burgers but unfortunately chose a metal mixing bowl to cook them.

As you can imagine the burgers burnt and he was left without any.

There are pictures on all the cupboard doors in the cookery room, clearly labelling all the equipment so the teacher is at a loss as to why he ended up with a metal mixing bowl.

He is a bit upset by this, although was not in any trouble. We thought it would be easier if you knew before he came home.

Kind regards,

Sue

I responded asking for a little bit more detail on how this may have happened given he should be receiving 25 hours of Learning Support Time. This was the response:

Dear Mr and Mrs Woolgar,

Sue has asked me to email you regarding Zac's practical lesson on Friday. The lesson was an assessment and all of the students were being observed, it was explained to them that they had to follow their plans that were completed in the previous lesson. All of the students were expected to work independently and to facilitate this all equipment in the practical room has been labelled and everything that students may need for the session was out for them to use.

When it was observed that Zac had selected the incorrect piece of equipment I did intervene and explained to him how to deal with this situation. We looked at his recipe together and discussed what he should have been using and how he could try to complete his practical work. I thought it would be unwise to make a big issue of the situation in front of the class as the students were working quietly. So the conversation was very calm and encouraging, as I wanted Zac to be able to complete the whole session without causing him any more stress. Zac hasn't failed the assessment, as this was not a pass/fail situation he will receive a level like the other students in the class.

Though Zac selected the incorrect piece of equipment to place on a hob – it was a stainless-steel bowl, which would not melt, or shatter during use unlike plastic or glass bowls. The intervention happened quickly enough that Zac was not at risk. The email from Mrs H is incorrect in that he didn't burn the burgers. The mixture was still mainly raw. We discussed the next steps that Zac could take in order for him to feel that he had accomplished something for himself by the end of the lesson.

Kind Regards

Miss H

Two weeks later this happened:

Hi Abbey

Just a quick note reference Zac and his cooking ingredients this morning: Zac completed in class a plan to cook a fish dish, this however had been changed and he brought ingredients to cook a pizza. This caused some confusion in lesson as Zac brought ingredients to make dough and not the scone base pizza that's in his booklet. This caused delay within the lesson and caused Zac to become anxious because he wasn't keeping up with the rest of the class. I did with the help of the teacher get the pizza ready to be cooked in the oven, but the pizza still wasn't ready to be taken out of the oven at the end of the lesson. This is for your information if Zac is worried or anxious when he comes home.

On a lighter note, Zac interacted well with others today during a French computer lesson, when another student tried to wind me up in a funny way. Zac joined in and became excited and laughed with the other boys. I did join in his laughter and was pleased he was able to express his delights.

Kind regards

K

The pizza that Zac made was delicious and better than any scone-based pizza or fish dish but we were glad when cookery at school was over.

Walt seemed to plod through his GCSE years; he had a couple of hiccups along the way. The worst being the day before he took his early sitting of GCSE maths exam, one of the senior staff members challenged him in the corridor about his haircut. Now we wouldn't have minded, had he not had the same haircut for the past 2 years but this kind of gave him a massive wobbly melt down at a key time in his life. He did pass the exam but after a lot of talking down by both his Mum and Dad. Walt went on to achieve 3 A levels and was offered a place at Buckingham University studying a BA (Hons) 2-year degree in History with Politics. It is safe to say he loves it.

Zac however, continued to struggle at school not academically but with the rules and boundaries that didn't appear to be logical to him.

Here are just a few of the issues we experienced:

Hi

Zac came home today saying that Mrs C was very angry this morning for putting their bikes in the 'usual' place. Both boys have said they feel uncomfortable putting their bikes in the main bike rack and while we understand there have been changes, this may affect the boy's start to the day. We would be grateful if you could explain why there has been a sudden change and why this has not been implemented gradually for them?

We look forward to your response.

Regards

Abbey and Colin Woolgar

A week later:

Hi Sue

Zac is still anxious about the parking of his bike. He has been told by Mrs C again that he is not allowed to park it where he has done for the last two years. Please can the reason for this be explained again to him, he is not happy about putting it in the main bike rack because of the 'other students'.

Many thanks.

Abbey and Colin Woolgar

Dear Mrs Woolgar,

Zac and Walt are allowed to leave their bikes where they always have done. Mrs C has agreed this now and both boys have been made aware.

Kind regards - Sue

The issue around where to park their bikes stopped shortly after I witnessed one of their fellow students attempt to push Walt off his bike. Now this wouldn't have been too bad had it not been on a bridge, which dropped down onto a busy dual carriageway and the mere fact that she bellowed "retard" at him at point of impact.

Zac also experienced some vile fellow students. He came home one day quite excitable as he had been asked to join some of his classmates at the local football pitch for a kick about. I was quite pleased that he wanted to go and join them. He told me where he was going and that he would probably be gone about an hour. He rapidly changed into some sports shorts; the elastic round the middle ones, a t-shirt and some trainers and off he went. Some thirty minutes later, he returned in floods of tears. I sat him down and asked what the matter was. He blubbed his way through what I can only describe as the most juvenile behaviour.

When Zac had arrived at the football pitch the other boys had been kicking the ball about. They didn't involve Zac in the game but one of them snuck up behind him and whipped down his shorts. Now in their defence, I suspect they thought it would only be his shorts that would come down but alas, his underwear came too. Now Zac was pretty good at naming and shaming in those days so when I asked him who had done this he told me the names. As every mother would, I cycled to the pitch and decided to have words. The trouser pulling young lad who I singled out, mainly because his mates, deserted him, no surprise there, was strongly asked how he would feel if the shoe had been on the other foot.

After about 10 minutes of putting the lad in the picture about how disgusted I was I cycled away. I didn't return straight home because I needed to calm myself down. When I did eventually return home though. Zac explained that the lad had been round and that he had apologised for his behaviour. I asked Zac what he had said. Zac said, "I'm sorry for what I did, can we be friends again?" I said and "what did you say?" Zac replied "I said I would think about it". I was very proud at this moment.

Then there was this from school:

Dear Mrs Woolgar,

Zac appears to be misplacing his pens and pencils at the moment and Kimberley has been providing him with her own spares. Unfortunately he, again, lost the spare pen that she lent him today so she felt it was appropriate to issue him with an 'E' for not having the correct equipment in school.

I had a chat with him at break to explain that we would not lend or give pens/pencils to other students and that Mrs V had been protecting him for some time but we had to issue the 'E' today to keep him in line with other students. He listened and actually apologised to Mrs V later in the day as he did become a bit 'stroppy' due to the 'E'.

Anyway, the reason for my email is to ask if you could provide pens and pencils that we could hold in school for either boy, at the start of September, should they misplace any items. By having a supply, we can avoid the 'E' that clearly upset him this morning but he was mature enough to understand and cope with my gentle chat. He happily left the Inclusion room at break time and continued to enjoy the rest of his day.

Kind regards

Sue

I replied:

Hi

Thank you for your e-mails.

I sat with Zac last night and looked through his pencil case. He did have at least two pencils and a pen in his pencil case along with a ruler, rubber, pencil crayons, his calculator and a pencil sharpener and so I can see why he was 'stroppy' as he would not have understood why an 'E' was issued, when he clearly had the right equipment had he been supported to check it or we had been notified sooner that he needed replacements. We are concerned that this has happened so close to the end of the school year as Zac will now worry about this over the summer, as he did last year. Last night he said he did not want to go to school and this was repeated again this morning, so we are quite concerned again. We will put a social story in place for Zac ready for next term on making sure he has the right equipment before he comes to school.

Regards

Abbey and Colin Woolgar

I think we sent at least one email to school a week to clarify or question a decision and get an explanation as to why this or that had happened. It often felt like I was banging my head against a brick wall.

I think the one Zac felt was most annoying was when he was put into the under-achiever group for PE. A group the school had designed for young people who didn't take any exercise or those who were overweight. Zac was attending hockey training twice a week, playing at least 2 matches at the weekend and has never been overweight. Not to mention the 2 dog walks he did a day and the fact he cycled to and from school. Who were we to question that school decision though?

I rather enjoyed it though when Zac did prove the school wrong. In 2014, 2 years prior to Zac doing his GCSE's the school requested a meeting to suggest that he wouldn't be suitable for their sixth form provision and that we should start to look elsewhere for him. This was a bit of a shock considering he hadn't even started to work towards his exams. They suggested he "just wouldn't achieve the necessary C grades." But I guess this was then also compounded by emails like this and we should have twigged at this point that this school was never going to be the right place for Zac:

Hi Mrs Woolgar,

I have had a response from Drama and the reason that Ms J feels that Zac would not be able to cope in GCSE Drama is down to the collaborative skills throughout the course.

Unit 3 of the course requires students to work in groups to devise their own performances – this is worth 40% of his overall GCSE. The remaining 60% is made up of collaborative workshops and reflective written responses to this process. She is also concerned in terms of his ability to accept constructive criticism from his peers or from the teacher guiding him through the process.

Ms J included the collaborative requirements as listed in the specification mark scheme.

There is a fluent use of strategies, elements and medium and a creative and collaborative involvement in all-practical tasks.

There is outstanding communication with other performers.

The sense of rapport with all members of the ensemble is outstanding.

Although we can't stop Zac from choosing Drama, it may turn out to harm his confidence and self-esteem if he were to choose this option.

Please let me know your thoughts, but once he starts he cannot withdraw, as discussed this morning.

Kind regards,

Sue

Zac absolutely loved drama and thrived on the stage, so we figured we should start to look for an alternative provision. Zac decided that he wanted to do Music Performance at Bedford College and after an interview and assessment he was offered a place from September 2016.

I should point out though that Zac had a fantastic Learning Support Assistant for his GCSE years, Mrs Goble, she really got him and supported him socially and academically and we are forever thankful for the time and effort she put into Zac when the school had already written him off.

On GCSE result day, we arrived at the school and I was dreading the disappointment of opening the envelope and the comparison with his brother's results that would then ensue. Especially when we had received and fought against decisions like this:

Dear Mr and Mrs Walters, [great spelling and checking of our name from an English teacher]

Zac achieved a D grade, which saw him 10 marks from a C grade. When put together with his controlled assessment, he got an overall C grade. It is my opinion that he would not achieve a C grade on the higher paper as the paper requires more advanced skills than Zac is capable of.

If he sits the higher paper he would not achieve anything higher than a D grade, and we feel it will cause him too much stress.

We feel it is much better to keep Zac on the foundation paper and work at securing that C grade which is so important for Zac's future.

Please do not hesitate to contact us should you have any concerns.

Kind regards – Mrs J

But to our shock and utter bewilderment the boy had done well! So well that he achieved, 3 B's in Music, English and Math's, 2 C's in Media and Geography and a D for History. These results are most probably because Mrs Goble had been an utter superstar. I marched Zac up to the sixth form sign up table on results day and insisted they offered him a place on their Music, Finance and Business courses. They were a little gob smacked.

And in hindsight making him go to school sixth form was the worst decision we ever forced. After 6 months Zac had lost all motivation to attend school, he disengaged with almost everything and we became increasingly worried about his self-confidence. We are pretty sure that the school had a large hand to play in this. Zac was we think made to feel quite unwelcome by the staff. I guess they didn't like the fact that they had pegged him all wrong. By the middle of the spring term of 2017 we requested a meeting to discuss the best way forward. The meeting was terrible and the final nail in the coffin for Zac's experiences in a school setting, but it made us realize that we needed to take control and make the move for Zac and boy was it a great move.

Zac decided that he would go to Bedford College and study ICT (or computing to you and me). He went to a taster session and absolutely loved it. He was very proud of a cable he made at the taster session and so he left it on the kitchen bench for me to admire but with no explanation. When I got home from work that evening, I assumed it was something that the dog had chewed in the lounge earlier in the day and promptly placed it in the bin, much to Zac's horror.

Zac's first day at College was a slight disaster. We had practiced going on the bus to and from Bedford a few times over the summer. Each journey to Bedford had to include a "nice drink" and a trip to

Pizza Express because there isn't a Chiquito in Bedford. On his first day, I walked him up to the Coach way Station with the dogs and as we approached he said "It's alright mum I can do this by myself". I was a little taken a back but said "OK, if you are sure?". The response came back "Yes I know which bus I am getting on, X5 to Cambridge". I left him, turned round and walked the dogs back towards home. After about 5 minutes of walking the Oxford bound X5 bus went past me and I had a sixth sense thought of "I do hope Zac didn't get on that bus" About 30 seconds later my phone rang:

"Mum . . . I think I am on the wrong bus"

"Did you get on the Oxford X5 bus Zac?"

"Yes I think so"

"OK get off at the train station and mum will come and pick you up, see you in a bit"

I ran home, telephoning Walt on my way.

"Walt, Mum's battery is just about to die please call Zac and check he understood that he should get off at the train station"

"OK"

I got home. Walt told me he had managed to get hold of Zac and that yes he would go to the train station.

I got straight in the car drove as quickly as I could to get to the train station only to be met with a very sweaty Zac and no X5.

I asked *"Zac why are you so sweaty?"*

"Well I got off the bus at the next stop and then there was another Cambridge X5 bus so I got on that one but then Walt called to tell me to go to the train station, so I have run [about a mile] to get here to meet you. Walt said you would be cross if I didn't" Of course, I wouldn't have been cross. I would have been very proud of him for self-correcting his journey error.

We drove as quickly as we could back to the Coachway to meet the bus Zac had tried to self-correct on. We laughed about how I needed to start to trust that he knew what he was doing. In typical style we pulled into the Coachway just as the bus was pulling out to go to Bedford. Good job Mum was working from home that day! I managed to get him to Bedford just in time for his first registration.

Thankfully this didn't deter Zac at all and he cracked the journey to and from College and by the first Parent's evening I heard words about Zac that hadn't been heard for a very long time in an educational setting *"He is an absolute pleasure and so intelligent"*

This continued well into the first year until the point when Zac lied to us. At the end of the term he told us he had a achieved a double distinction. WARNING Proud Mum moment: He hadn't achieved that at all. What he had achieved was a double distinction star - only the highest grade obtainable in his first year of BTEC study. Safe to say in his second year Zac smashed it again and achieved a triple distinction star, the highest grade achievable and was given an award at the Bedford College Achievement Ceremony in December 2019.

In July 2019 Zac went for an interview at Buckingham University to study Computing. I took him along but told him he could do it by himself. As he left the car I said *"if they ask to see Mum say that I know about the fees and how it works because Walt is already here"*. *"OK"* said Zac and off he went looking very smart in his waistcoat, shirt and formal trousers. I on the other hand looked pretty terrible. I was wearing . . . dare I say it my lined Crocs, some scruffy ¾ length jeans and a t-shirt that had seen better days. I was also sporting a rather nice large bruise on my chin from playing hockey the week before. I sat in what turned out to be a very hot car for about an hour waiting for him to return. Then my phone rang:

"Hi mum, it's me Zac"

"Hi Zac, how you doing?"

"I am ok, a lady wants to talk to you about money"

"OK can you tell the lady that I already know about the fees and the grants available because of Walt"

Muffled microphone

"Mum she really wants to talk to you can you meet us at the entrance please?"

Phone goes dead.

I dragged my by now very hot and sweaty body out of the car and hoped that the breeze would cool me down a bit on the quick hop to the entrance.

The lady greeted me and said, *"We would like to offer Zac a place on the course"*

"Oh that's great, thank you"

"Now let me just explain the finance"

"But I know about the finance as Walt is here"

"Well Zac will get the high achievers award on top of the 5 counties grant that you will receive and you will receive a sibling discount"

"Oh that's great thanks"

"And of course a lady in your situation will also be eligible for other financial help too"

"I'm sorry, what?"

"You know a lady in your situation"

"Sorry I don't know what you mean?"

"You know a lady who . . . " [She looked me up and down a couple of times]

I eventually clicked what she meant, *"Oh no, sorry I work full time"*

"...and this?" [Pointing to my chin]

"Oh this I got playing hockey"

Bless her, I am not 100% sure what she had assumed but it really wasn't what I was expecting. We decided that at that point it would be good to just finish the conversation as rapidly as possible and leave.

The journey to Buckingham involves doing the same X5 coach journey in reverse. The only problem with getting on the wrong bus is that it only stops in Bedford before heading to St Neots and then finally Cambridge. Zac luckily has only once managed to get on the wrong X5 and thankfully he got off just before it left the Coachway.

Zac had a bit of a rocky start at University and we thought it wasn't going to work. He went through a period of doubting his ability and we thought that we were seeing the Zac of old secondary school. We arranged appointments for counseling, with our GP and meetings for other educational provisions just in case. But then a few weeks into the first term he came running down the stairs shouting *"Mum, Mum look!"* He showed me an email, which read:

Dear Zachary

Your result for your first assignment is 100%.

Keep up the good work.

Buckingham University

Now sometimes in these moments the amount of stress and work that can be caused by Zac's anxiety can only be addressed with a sarcastic reply, which this time was:

"Next time please try harder Zac, that's result really isn't good enough."

He did of course see the funny side of this. He continues to have his ups and downs but luckily they are more up than down but we still feel like an emotional support crutch. My only concern is that one day he or Walt for that matter might ask me to read or check their work and I will be honest now there is no way I will be able to make head nor tail of it.

She'll never know

Of course school wasn't all bad. When Zac was 15 this happened:

"Mum, I need to talk to you!" Bathroom door shuts behind him. *"Can this wait Zac, I am kind of in the middle of being naked"* I reply.

"No, I must talk to you now".

"Go on then, I am listening"

"Well you see my willy touched my music score".

"Pardon"

"Well today I have to hand in my music to Miss ready for my GCSE practical next week and you see well my willy touched it"

"Well, how did your willy manage to touch the music Zac?"

"That doesn't matter, it just did"

"Okay so did your willy leave any marks on the music?" God knows why I asked this question but I did!

"No, why would it do that?"

"Well you know, you didn't…"

"Of course I didn't' dot dot dot"

We had come up with a code word for masturbating which became lovingly known as dot dot dotting. Goodness knows why we decided on that, I guess it was just easier to call it that then wanking, masturbating or knocking one out.

I had always said that I would always use the correct terminology because many years ago when I was about 7 or 8 our neighbour told me that her son, James, had to go into hospital to have his "taily" cut off. She meant of course that he was going to be circumcised for medical reasons but for me this just conjured up all sorts of images in my head when I met poor James in the street. It would have been easier if she had used the correct medical terms but I guess she thought I could relate better to thinking boys were like monkeys with large tails swinging behind them.

The conversation with Zac continued with me saying *"Why are you so worried then?"*

"Well if my willy has touched the music then Miss is touching my willy"

Without laughing hysterically I said *"And why do you think that Zac?"*

"Well my willy touched the music so therefore, Miss will be touching where my willy was, so she would in effect be touching my willy. Will she need to wash her hands?"

At that point I had to giggle and I just said *"If you don't tell her about your willy touching the paper she will never know that she is touching where it was. But you will know so you can keep that as your secret"*. That seemed to do the trick and off he went upstairs to get ready for school leaving me in peace.

At the age of 18 this happened.

Bath time is never boring in my house. For some reason the boys have no inhibitions about wandering round the house naked. This being said, they also have no inhibitions about seeing their mother naked either. When Walt started studying at University the subjects he was learning were exciting to him and so in-depth that he felt he should try and discuss them with us, usually at the most inopportune moments. I was laying in the bath relaxing, with my head under the water, eyes closed, when I sat up and opened my eyes I was presented with a fully naked Walt. He had one leg up on the bath while brushing his teeth with his genitals nearly in my face.

"Mum, did you know that Rasputin was a very bad man?"

"No Walt, I didn't"

"Well let me explain . . . "

"Rasputin was some sort of weird monk who had sex with a lady who was married to a very important man and well because they had sex that meant that Russia was in trouble"

Now my history has never been great and I wouldn't know if this was correct or not but I feared his lecturer may have hysteria if he wrote this in any 1500 word assignment. As all good mums do, they get out of the bath and say *"Alexa play Rasputin by*

Boney M". Of course this wasn't the best way of clarifying the historical significance of Rasputin but it did remove the swinging genitals from my face so I could get out of the bath and it provided a distraction from a deep historical discussion and moved us onto a subject I am much better at fielding - terrible music.

WARNING: proud Mum moment alert - Walt did submit his assignment on the subject and he achieved 71% of which of course I am claiming part of for my Boney M clarification.

Work

Of course education isn't everything, it is only really one part of a person and we have always tried to encourage Zac and Walt to be rounded in what they achieve so that they have plenty to talk about at job interviews. Although we made the tough choice to remove Zac from sixth form earlier than planned, we did encourage him to get a job to fill in what would have been a very long summer.

I have always been a big believer in "it's not what you know, it's who you know" and getting Zac a job on his own merit would have been quite a challenge. Luckily I knew someone, a lovely lady called Emma, who knew someone who was one of the managers at the local theme park. She kindly sent Zac's details in on our behalf and within a couple of days he had an interview, induction and a start date.

Zac has a great job for him, which involves most of his time working on his own sweeping, cleaning and tidying the park. Walt on the other hand has a job there, because his brother asked for him (again it's not what you know) but works in one of the cafes serving people or cooking. Walt often comes home and imparts stories of how grumpy customers are. They did let Walt work in the waterpark section at one point but he didn't like that very much because "it smelt bad" and "the fat kids kept getting stuck on the slides and I had to tell them off".

Zac's best story of all time, was when he was asked to pick up all of the disposable BBQs and empty the bins in the chalets. Both boys are very good at following instructions as long as they are clear but thinking outside of the instruction can be a bit of a struggle. Zac had done exactly what he had been asked, he had placed all of the disposable BBQs in his black dustbin sack and then had started to go from chalet to chalet to empty the dustbins. The only problem was he hadn't made sure that the BBQs were out completely. The more rubbish Zac put in the bags, the more fuel he was starting to add to the soon to be fire. Zac explained that he had put his bag down by the entrance to the chalet and he went to hunt for the bin because the people who had been in that particular chalet were "really quite disgusting". Just as he found the bin, a voice shouted, "Zac for fucks sake, what are you doing?" Zac said he turned to see a lot of smoke and the black bag melting. Zac prefers now to sweep the park and only empty the easy park bins, they are apparently a lot less hazardous!

Work has been my way of putting my head in the sand when times have been tough at home. Not that it gets really tough but sometimes it is nice to use my grey matter for things other than creating schedules, lists and social stories and repetition.

In 2012 our dog Spencer tore his cruciate ligament. This is a story in itself but for now I will just focus on the work aspect of this story. Now a torn cruciate ligament might not sound that significant but when you decide that for a time you should primarily be a housewife/mother and money becomes tight it becomes really significant. Especially when you don't have pet insurance because you decided that instead of paying out £70 a month you would put it to one side. Of course saving money didn't happen and then you receive a bill for some £3500. I decided that I should find some part time work in an actual place of work.

This of course would be a massive step for all of us because I had always either been able to either work from home or be my own boss and work around Colin's hours. So I dusted off my CV and set about finding a real job that would pay for the dog's leg. It happened quite quickly and the job was perfect, 10am – 3pm Monday to Friday and only about 15 minutes drive from home. The interview went well. Of course when they asked, "Why do you want the job?" I didn't reply, "Just to fix the dog's leg," I made some long-winded story up about how I was ready to get back on the career ladder and they offered me the job. I started 4 days later, not much time to prepare the boys for the change but just enough time to make sure I could prepare myself.

The boys didn't seem bothered at all about the slight changes to their routine and were more concerned by the mere thought that this could potentially mean more money to buy video games. My primary concern was fixing Spencer's leg and then going back to be a full time housewife/mother, I am still waiting for that bit to happen, as I am clearly not cut out to be a homemaker because I go to work and get my head well and truly stuck in the sand.

Within 9 months of starting the job I was asked to take on a more senior role managing the company's IT and Communications. At last my Mum could be proud of me for actually having a job title that sounded a bit like my degree, it had only taken me 19 years. I was given the grand title of Technical and Communications Manager.

This role brought me many challenges and a lot of laughs but in the end it became too intense and I was spending way too much time focusing on work and not on my young gentlemen so I needed to find a new role that would provide me with more of a home/work life balance. This took me some time and was an incredibly hard decision to make but when the role did come along that looked like it could fit the part I needed to really prepare the young gentlemen.

The new role was in an area with poor mobile phone reception, which meant it was difficult to receive phone calls or text messages from the boys. The boys had previously both become quite good at texting and calling when there was a problem.

The funniest and most memorable phone call was when me and Colin were walking the dogs on a nice hot summers evening. We had started to do family Saturday cooking sessions. This involved me working with either Zac or Walt on the main course and Colin working with the other on dessert. The boys always picked spaghetti as the main. Spaghetti is a favourite after fish fingers so this particular Saturday they had suggested that we walked the dogs while they cooked the tea. Novel, and we thought, quite relaxing. Then the phone rang.

"Mum, I can't get the tomato puree out of the tube."

"Have you opened it?"

"Yes"

"OK have you squeezed it?"

"Yes, I squeezed it really hard and . . . Oh dear"

Phone goes dead.

We walked home really quickly, as there was no reply or the engaged tone when we tried to call back.

When we walked into the kitchen an explosion of tomato puree greeted us as far as the eye could see. Walt had indeed opened the tomato puree. It was a new tube. A tube, which needed piercing which of course he hadn't done and its a science fact that when you squeeze a tube that is sealed, it will find the weakest link and escape that way. In this case it had come straight out of the other end - at full force. The plus side was the spaghetti hadn't burnt too badly - Yes, you can burn spaghetti with a gas ring. All in all it was quite a tasty bolognaise.

Another but far scarier call was when Walt went AWOL at the gym. Walt loves the gym. He wants to have "big muscles to impress the ladies" as he says, not that he even notices when they look at him but maybe one day his guns will impress a partner. Each evening after school he would take himself off to the gym (it is right next door) and Zac would go home to see the dog. Spencer had left us but the good news was that we paid for his leg and we managed to spoil him rotten and take out insurance for the rest of his time with us because I had a job that would pay for any more leg emergencies.

At 16:50 my mobile phone rang. It was Zac

"Er hi mum"

"Hi Z how you doing?"

"Well, you see Walt hasn't come home yet"

"Right, do you know where he is?"

"No"

Slight panic set in

"Have you tried to call him?"

"Yes"

"And . . . ?"

"Well . . . he didn't answer"

"Ok so . . . , did you try and ring him again?"

"No"

"Ok, mum will try and call him and I will let you know what is happening"

"Ok"

Phone goes dead. No goodbye. No I'll keep trying to call. No I will let you know if he comes home. We are still working on how to end a phone call. There are so many possible combinations so think this is going to be a struggle.

I try Walt's mobile. No reply. I try again. No reply.

Panic sets well and truly in. Called again, still no reply.

"Hi Zac, I can't get him either, could you walk up to school with Percy and see if you can see him"

"Ok"

Phone goes dead. No goodbye. No I'll keep trying to call. No I will let you know if I find him.

I sit and wait. It was the longest wait I think I had ever had. I counted the steps that Zac would have to take to get to school. I had done it about a thousand times. I even factored Percy doing a poo on the way into the timing before I tried to call Zac again. I was speed dialing Walt's phone as I counted the steps but still nothing.

There are many things that go through your head at this point but what had actually happened never entered my head. I called Zac again.

"Hey matey chops, how you doing? Any sign of Dub?"

"Nope, but Percy did a poo"

"Ok are you at the school?"

"Yes"

"And you definitely didn't walk past Dub on the way up to school?"

"Nope"

"Ok, you go home, pickle and mum will come home"

My colleagues at this point had cottoned on to what was going on and had also started to get concerned. At this point it was 17:20 way past going home from work time. I didn't know what to do, if I left work and the hospital called to tell me he was there, of course this is where I had put him now in my head, I wouldn't be able to answer my phone while driving in rush hour traffic. I called the school as I started to leave.

Now you'd think that most staff would have gone home by 17:00 but luckily that evening I managed to get hold of someone. I explained my absolute panic and predicament and suggested that could we perhaps have a look around for him at school and at the gym. The very nice staff member (I don't say that often about the staff at that school) said of course.

I waited again what felt like forever for my phone to ring. I checked on Zac made sure he had returned home. He simply asked, *"What's for tea?"* when I called. Then the call came from the school. Thankfully they had found him.

It transpires that what had happened was that Walt had arrived at the gym followed his normal routine of:

    1. Get changed into tight fitting gym kit

2. Chuck all day clothes into an already full rucksack of A level school folders and stuff. He won't ever empty the bag, just in case. I am never sure what the just in case bit actually means but I won't put my hands in there for fear of finding a banana skin or worse still a condom from sex ed.
3. Cram back in the locker
4. Lock the locker and place key .....

It was step 4 that had caused the challenge. The difficulty you have when wearing tight fitting gym kit is that the pockets are probably too tight to put keys in securely. Add to this some Walt's "can't be bothered to take time to put said key in pocket" - et voila disaster strikes.

Yep Walt had lost his key. Now most people would go to Reception and explain in an apologetic manner. No. Walt decided to sit between the lockers for some 2 hours and either wait for the key to magically appear or hope that he could use the power of his mind to open the door. Neither of these happened. Luckily when the nice school person arrived she was able to ask the Receptionist for the master key and his clothes magically appeared.

When the boys were much younger I had read the book "The Curious Incident of the Dog in the Night-Time" and thought that some of the tales in it were a bit farfetched, especially when the main character stayed in the underpass for some time. Well this was Walt's way of showing me that it really wasn't farfetched at all.

The week before I started the job with no mobile phone access I decided that I would put some boundaries in place to practice a lack of contact. This worked quite well and both boys seemed to get to grips with not ringing me to find out what was for tea or more importantly when was I next going shopping to buy fish fingers.

Picture a very nice country pub in the middle of nowhere, delicious food, quiet and very comfortable seats. My line manager, Sarah, and myself were going through what work I needed to hand over before I left when my phone started to ring. I placed it upside down. Sarah said *"Are you not going to answer that I think it's Zac?"*

"No, I have told them this is good practice for when I start my new job next week"

"OK if you are sure"

The phone kept ringing every 30 minutes or so. In total I think I missed about 6 calls from Zac. In the end Sarah said, *"Maybe you should answer it, it could be really important"*

Now I am pretty stubborn but whilst not answering the phone there had been some things that had raced through my mind like:

1. Had Walt lost his locker key again?
2. Had he run out of fish fingers?
3. Had the hoover stopped working?
4. Or even worse had the mop stopped working?

What I hadn't planned for was this . . .

"Oh hello mum, yeah sorry I kept ringing but you see well there has been an incident"

"Go on"

"Well you see Rufus . . ."

Rufus is our new Gordon Setter - completely bonkers, slightly on the spectrum but very loveable. Zac desperately wanted another Gordon Setter because he felt that Percy was very much Walt's dog. Of course Rufus and Percy are still very much mine and Colin's dogs!

"Yes Zac what has Rufus done?"

"Well you see Rufus . . . "

"Yes Zac, what has Rufus done"

I had all sorts of visions of him disappearing over the horizon as Zac opened the door to a delivery person or worse still chasing said delivery person.

"Well Rufus has had an incident"

Some months earlier Zac and Rufus had an incident in my kitchen. Mornings before school were always hectic. This particular morning was no different. I had gone upstairs to get dressed ready to assist with the school run leaving Zac downstairs eating his breakfast. When I returned to the kitchen I noticed spots of blood all over Zac's white pyjama top.

"Zac where has that blood come from?"

"What blood?"

The blood on your top?"

Zac had no clue. Then I spotted blood on the ceiling, up the walls, splattered across the benches and across the kitchen units. The quicker I tried to clear it up the more it kept appearing, fresher, redder and faster. I couldn't work out where it was coming from it was like the famous Psycho shower scene. I then realised that it was coming from Rufus. Gordon Setters have very long tails with very long feathering, which combined with their happy and energetic disposition can be quite a disadvantage. Yes the blood was spraying out from a very waggy tail like some sort of macabre paint splatter brush. When I realised where it was coming from I asked Zac if he knew what had happened. Of course he said in that moment that he had no clue. I took Rufus to the vet, after strapping a lot of bandage around his tail. The vet examined the tail and then explained that he had lost the very end tip end from his tail and that he must have experienced a sharp trauma of some description. I asked Zac when I returned if he had remembered what had happened and he said *"Oh yes, Rufus did get his tail shut in the door"*. Yes that would explain it. I asked, *"Did Rufus yelp?"* *"No, mum he was fine"*. Henceforth this is why we now lovingly refer to him as Doofus.

"Zac, what kind of incident?"

"Well you see Rufus did go in my bathroom"

"Yes"

"And I had done a very big poo"

"Yes and what did Rufus do?"

"Well Rufus did eat the poo"

"Sorry, he did what, why did you not flush it down the toilet?"

"Well the poo was too big and it got stuck. I left it in the toilet. And Rufus did come along and eat the poo."

"Has Rufus been sick?"

"No Rufus has put poo all round the house"

"Sorry, he has done what?"

"Rufus did put poo all round the house, he did drink the poo out of the toilet and then shook all round the house"

"Er ok, and how long ago did this happen?"

"When I first called you"

"Ok so have you cleaned it up?"

"Well I tried"

"OK I am on my way home, see you soon."

"OK"

Phone goes dead.

I drove home thinking I was coming home to utter poo carnage. Instead I walked into what appeared to be a very clean poo free zone. I was slightly shocked. Zac was looking very pleased with himself. *"See I did clean all the poo up by myself"*. I couldn't disagree with him at all he had done a rather splendid job especially when he graphically described the size of the poo and the horror that unfolded with Rufus's poo filled slobber chops.

The next morning though was a slightly different story, and I'd already forgotten about the day before. I went into the boys' bathroom, tidied up the towels, not from the floor like your typical teenager but from their precariously tucked in state from between the radiator pipes, only to discover a 2 centimeter brown splodge above them. I scratched said brown dollop and then yes . . . sniffed it! Yes, yes it really was the remnants of Zac's giant poo trapped in Rufus's slobber just like a fly trapped in amber from the Jurassic period.

As you can see blood, sweat and poo still feature in our lives quite heavily.

He's 17 ½

Hockey is still a big part of our lives. In 2016, I wrote to England Hockey simply asking if they knew of any local hockey teams that provided any Special Educational Needs groups. They responded telling me about a scheme they run but at the same time asked if I would write an article on ASD and hockey. I cheated. I stole the chapter from my own book "Let the Teenage Years begin" and they published it on Facebook and their website. I wasn't expecting to be tweeted though by Helen Richardson-Walsh, MBE she wrote:

H Richardson-Walsh @ h_richardson8
Nothing like a bit of sibling rivalry (pumped up arm emoji) Heart warming to hear Abbey's story – all the best to her Zac & Walt #inclusion #autism @EnglandHockey

The boys weren't impressed but I thought it was pretty cool. I am getting way too old and slow to actually play hockey but I love the social side of it; having the excuse to go on road trips to exotic places like Slough, having pre or post match (or both) McDonalds, and of course not to mention the occasional drinking that goes with it. The obligatory End of Season dinner used to provide me with the opportunity to embarrass them both with my Justin Bieber dance moves but they soon cottoned on that moving to another club meant they would no longer have to endure this type of punishment. I have met so many lovely people playing hockey, some of whom I would call very good friends and I hope that this will be something the boys will continue to do when university is finished because hockey players really are an eclectic bunch.

The hockey training session that still haunts me though is Halloween 2017. I had totally embarrassed my 2 young gentlemen by dressing up as Jack Skellington from The Nightmare Before Christmas. I had full-face paint on and told them that I would be attending my own hockey training session dressed this way and that if they wanted a lift to training, some 30 minutes away from my own, then they would have to put up with having embarrassing Mum that evening. They tried desperately to get me to change by saying things like what if we break down on the M1, what would people think, this of course wouldn't have stopped me in the slightest and to be honest probably only encouraged me.

The boys were successfully dropped off at their session and I drove, without breaking down on the M1, all the way to my training session, trained and then drove all the way back up the M1, without having to stop. I got to the school where the boys trained and thought I know I will now go and be full on embarrassing mum and wait for them by the side of the pitch. For some reason as I approached, Walt came running out of the changing room. He didn't acknowledge me, even though I waved and shouted *"Hi Walt"*. After training, we all went back to the car; they walked a few paces in front, so as not to be seen with the fake Jack.

Now what you need to know here is that Walt never wants to sit in the back seat of the car when the front seat is free. I should have known something was wrong when Walt said *"Zac you sit in the front".* At first I said, *"Oh that's nice Walt, Zac can be DJ and choose the music he likes on the way home"*, a grunt sounded from the back. Hockey is a winter sport, mainly, and so as we got into the car the heater went on full blast. As we started to drive away from the pitch I could smell something odd. I asked the mum question *"Boys have either of you trodden in something?"* After a bit of shuffling about both replied no. I checked my own. The smell was getting stronger; the more movement there was in the car and the warmer the heater made it. We drove a bit further down the road, naively thinking that maybe, just maybe it was coming from outside. Nope the smell got stronger and stronger the more we drove. Then Walt said *"Oh dear, I think it is me."*

I drove as quickly as I could home asking, *"Why do you think it is you?"* over and over again. The reply finally came *"I don't think I wiped properly."* When we got home, I was glad it was dark so that I couldn't see the horror that had unfolded in Walt's hockey shorts and more upsettingly on the back seat of my car. It took me back to the day that we experienced Thomas and the Poo but this time it was far worse - this was adult poo.

Now I know my 2 very good friends and hockey teammates Sue and Jo would say that this is nothing compared to some of my antics both on and off the pitch. At the last training session I attended we got a terrible case of the giggles and it was cold and we ran a lot and all I will say is that since that fateful evening I now have to wear a safety Tena Lady at all times at matches just in case.

This season the boys have been less interested in hockey. No ot because of the poo story but because university studies have been given priority. Their choice not ours. They do still play with Colin and me in the garden and occasionally play for local teams but when Walt started at Buckingham University he was slightly disappointed that there wasn't a hockey team. Buckingham had so many other advantages one of which was that he could try something a bit different. On registration day we went to chat to the polo team captain, a great guy called Houzafa. We explained that Walt had some good hand eye coordination skills developed while playing hockey but that he had only ever ridden a pony once at the grand old age of 6 and that my only experience of polo was watching Pretty Woman. Houzafa explained that they ran a polo taster session and that Walt should come along to see if he liked it. To prepare we watched a couple of polo training videos where people sat on wooden horse shaped boxes and swung mallets about to practice passing the ball. I told Walt that this is what he would be doing at the taster session. How wrong was I?

Within the space of a few weeks Walt represented Buckingham University in an indoor University polo tournament near Warwick. I stood watching a match taking place between Oxford and the Royal Veterinary College because Houzafa, Sam and Walt had all gone to warm up and as I turned around to look down onto the warm up area there is my son galloping, yes galloping, swinging his mallet above his head and looking like a real polo player. I think the very expensive polo boots and whip helped but he is happy. This year he is Captain of the polo team and socially that's a pretty steep learning curve for someone with ASD but we are still hopeful that one day he might meet his pretty woman.

Sex Ed

Sex education has changed since I was at school quite significantly. In 1980 I remember sitting in a darkened classroom while Mr Nice, he really wasn't nice at all (in fact he had it in for me within the first 2 hours of being in his class because my brother had clearly paved the way for me) talked through some oil painting images of a man and a woman cuddling with no clothes on. I say cuddling I am sure they were doing more than that but when you are 9 years old it still really just boils down to that. I still remember thinking that to have a naked cuddle you really had to have a great deal of facial hair. This was reinforced horribly when I came upon a copy of The Joy of Sex that my parents had in their beside drawer a couple of years later. When I was in my early teens the only other sex ed was based on talking to the boys separately from the girls and explaining all about periods. This was fine as long as you hadn't already had your period for the last few years and the session just became an excuse to have a giggle with your friends at the back of the class.

I was therefore quite interested to see how they addressed the subject with the young people of the Millennium generation. The school invited all of the Year 9 parents to a briefing. On the day of the briefing I realised I hadn't responded to the invitation and really I should go to help my own 2 Millennium boys understand the complex nature of the topics they would be covering and that if I was able to sing from the same hymn sheet this would enhance their understanding. Also when the boys had been in Year 7 I had witnessed the Year 9's walking home from school blowing condoms up and flicking them in each other's faces so thought it may be a good idea to reinforce with the boys that this really wasn't how they were to be used. That being said I was also concerned and wanted to raise my issue of "why do you issue condoms to young people at the tender age of 13 when the legal age of sex in the UK isn't until 16?"

When I rang the school reception to book myself in, apologising profusely for my late notification, I was somewhat shocked at the eagerness of the receptionist to give me a place. It all became clear when I awkwardly arrived at the school. First of all the Caretaker had no idea where the briefing was being held. After walking round for 10 minutes to find out where the 300 plus parents were, I was expecting to be there, the Caretaker announces that it was being held in a classroom on the second floor and he would take me there. In I walk expecting, the room to be full of 30 parents and classrooms along the corridor to be replicating the same briefing, no I was greeted by one lady and a couple of parents. Now when I say a couple, they were a divorced couple that it quite clearly became clear that this had been a very messy end to said relationship. They spent most of the time scoring points off each other when the lady doing the briefing would say "and does your son talk to you about these things?" To which the ex-husband would respond in unison with the ex-wife "he talks to me about that but I know he doesn't talk to you about it". Awkward.

I sat listening to how they are going to explain the importance of finding the opposite sex attractive not only for their looks but for their personality by giving them pretend money and asking them to buy parts of a lady or man depending on their preference. This in itself raised a whole bunch of weird linking concepts in my head including having to explain to the boys that this was not in any way linked to prostitution.

Then the speaker moved onto the subject of condoms and that they would give all of the children a condom and they would demonstrate how this was put on using a vegetable. Yes a vegetable. I had to ask "What type of vegetable?" The reply came back, "well usually a carrot but occasionally we use a courgette or a parsnip". Knowing that these are 2 of the boy's least favourite vegetables I figured that this would be a mental contraceptive image in itself.

The day arrived of the vegetable condom session. As usual I walked the dogs up to meet the boys halfway home. Killing 2 birds with one stone, dogs exercised, boys' day discussed. I asked *"So how was putting the condoms on a vegetable today?"*

Complete silence and a blank look were returned.

I asked *"Did you learn about condoms today?"*

"Oh yes" then silence.

"Well what vegetable did you have to put it on?"

Again silence and both returned a blank look.

"Did you put it on a carrot?"

"No"

"Did you put it on a courgette?"

"No"

"Did you put it on a parsnip?"

"No"

"Did you put it on a marrow?" – I thought maybe there had been a shortage of suitably sized vegetables that day.

"No"

"Well, was it a banana?" Maybe they thought fruit with a bend would be more realistic that day.

"No of course not, don't be silly we put it on a vibrator of course. Do you have one of those Mum?"

At that point I decided that I would ask the age-old Mum distraction question *"So what do you fancy for tea tonight?"*

We haven't broached the subject again. I am still having nightmares about discovering my own mother's vibrator at the age of 10; my brother caught me with it under the bed because I thought it was a torch!

We are yet to really experience the boys having a girlfriend. Walt tried to date a girl at the age of 16. He was very attentive taking one particular girl out for coffee, Frankie and Benny's and an impromptu walk around our local parkland with the dogs. He organised the "dates" and called her pretty much every day for a chat. This went on for the whole of the summer holidays. Then one evening he came downstairs, just after the start of the new term, absolutely mortified that the girl he had liked had announced on Facebook that she was now in a relationship with another boy. He was heartbroken and I think he has vowed not to be interested in girls until he has finished studying. Most parents would say ok that's very sensible but deep down I know he really wants to find that one special friend again.

I text Walt, on my way home, a few weeks ago asking him to do a couple of extra jobs for me. I knew he had read the message because my phone is very clever and it tells me the message has been delivered and then read. I got home and found Walt hadn't started what I had asked him to do. I asked him if he had read the message. He did what most teenagers would in this situation and lied by saying *"What message?"* Now you might be thinking that's normal. For Walt this was the first time he had tried to lie, so my first reaction was that I was quite proud of him for lying, my second reaction was one of frustration. I called it out; *"Walt, I know you read it because my phone showed me you read it, have you just lied to me?"* The reply *"Er yes."* My third reaction was to get cross. I decided to take my crossness out on the ironing and within a few minutes Walt appeared with a letter apologising for his lie. Except it wasn't really an apology, what it said made me very sad.

Walt wrote:

Hi Mum

I am writing to you to let you know how lonely I am. I really need some friends and in particular a girlfriend but I don't know how to do this. Can you help me please? I try really hard sometimes but I really don't know what to do.

Walt

Dating now is so different to when me and Colin did it. We had to use public telephone boxes to call each other, which demonstrated our commitment to each other and there was none of this swipe left or swipe right business or social media stalking or worse pictures of genitals that goes on today. But I felt ready for this moment because a very nice young man at work called Charlie had helped me out. He had helpfully told me to keep the boys away from Tinder and Plenty of Fish and to go for something like Bumble.

I did my research and found that Bumble had a bee as a logo. Walt has always liked bees so I thought this might well be the right route to go with. As a punishment for lying I told him he must download the app and find a girlfriend. He did this very reluctantly. I of course supervised the proceedings not just because I wanted to keep him safe but because this was something completely alien to me. I have only ever seen a lady on the train doing the Tinder swipe. She had spotted her current boyfriend on there and proceeded to chastise him for this via text to her friend. Pot kettle black sprung to mind because she was clearly swiping both ways.

Walt, however, decided after hiding up in his bedroom for about an hour, after I was satisfied that he knew which direction to swipe, that this was not for him as the girls on the app either did drugs or wanted sex. For now Walt is content with waiting for the right girl and a monthly "Titty biscuit" which one of my colleagues, Yvette, brings down from Scotland. These of course, are really known as Empire Biscuits but when you have twins and you are given 2 to bring home and you place them side-by-side for consumption they do look rather like a pert set of boobs.

For Mothers Day last year, I received a lovely homemade card. But this time I was presented with a card which showed me just how much they loved me rather than wishing me a happy Mother's Day. It read:

Mummykins (inserted in a big red heart shape), this is what they sarcastically call me but I actually quite like it
Underneath - *Happy Valentines Day!!!*

I opened it up expecting it to say something like ha ha just kidding but no it said:

To Mum
Happy Valentines Day
Love Walt and Zac
PS I did not know what to draw but I hope you appreciate it

On the back was a drawing of Rufus and Percy.

One saying *RAOOOOOOOO* and the other saying *Woof x 5 hundred* and a quiz saying *you need to guess which one is which?*

I was more than happy with that but when they realised what they had done we all had a giggle about it but I reminded them that they should try hard not to muddle things up on Valentine's Day if they find girlfriends.

Driving

We always wanted the boys to be as independent as possible and so learning to drive was a given. When I was 17 my mum paid for 10 driving lessons, which I absolutely hated. After about 6 lessons I pretty much chucked in the towel. I had a break for about 6 months and then tried again with a different instructor - this time I found it a little easier. However, on the day of my first driving test, I had the worst case of shakiest clutch leg. Failed that one. The second test involved the same examiner coming out to greet me so I automatically decided I had failed before I even got into the car. And well the third time, same examiner, so it figured I would fail again. After that I left driving for about 2 years. Then my Mum decided to encourage me to take it up again. Changing instructors and test centres made a massive difference and within a few weeks I had passed my test. My mum bought me my first car a Fiat 126, which Colin hated, mainly because he felt he constantly had to fix it but I absolutely loved it. I have had numerous car accidents in my life, some my fault some other peoples. This I believe qualifies me as the world's worst passenger, even when Colin is driving. I can often be heard shouting "braking, braking, braking" at the top of my voice much to his annoyance.

From a really early age Walt in particular, was adept at video game driving simulations. The only problem was they would get very excited when they drove vehicles off road. The excitement levels, mainly a good old bounce and flap, would really get going when they drove vehicles off the edge of cliffs.

At 16 we applied for their Provisional Driving Licence so that we could book their Driving Theory Tests as soon after their 17th birthday as we could. We downloaded the DVSA theory app and booked a set of driving lessons with the AA. They turned 17 on the Sunday and were taking their first theory test the following Saturday. They both failed the first time round but undeterred we booked the next available slot. At this time, I began working towards my Category C (Lorry licence) and the Driver Qualification Card, which involved a lot of the same theory as the boys so I could test them to help them and me. I would ask them all sorts of weird highway code questions like "*What does a person walking down the side of the road carrying a red light mean?*" They of course responded with "*Is that like the red windows in Amsterdam mum?*" which of course we all know it isn't and that it is really the sign for an organised walk.

The day of the second theory test came. Colin and me dropped them off and went for a cheeky Wetherspoons breakfast before the nerve-wracking walk back to collect them. I say nerve-wracking. I think we were more concerned about how we would cope if one passed and the other didn't. When we approached them just outside the Test Centre they both looked glum so we were expecting the worst but to our delight they had both passed and they were just cross because they had had to wait for us.

We rang the insurance company to find out how much it would cost to put them on my car insurance so that we, I say we, I mean Colin here, could take them out on practice drives. When the very nice lady at the insurance company had stopped laughing and gasping for breath she said *"to put them on your car, your premium will increase to £10,516 per annum"*. You'd think I was driving a Ferrari for that but really I'm not. We decided that we should invest and buy the boys their own car. We ended up at our favourite place to buy a car, Car Giant. Colin was adamant that the boys would be learning to drive in either a Volkswagen Up or a Skoda Citigo, he had spent hours pouring over the internet. But no, instead, history repeated itself and calling to us from the corner of Car Giant was a fantastic Fiat – this time a Panda. Colin wasn't too keen. Now however, he thinks it is the most fun you can have in a car. Of course the insurance for this was a tenth of the price we had been quoted for mine for them both so it was a no brainer.

Walt decided that he would be the first to try for his practical, sadly he failed and was gutted. Zac was a little more hesitant but eventually put in for his test. On test day I asked to work from home so I could see him off and console him when he returned. Off he went and I paced about like a cat on a hot tin roof for most of the morning. When I heard the car pull up I looked out the window. Zac looked glum. I ran to the front door, his instructor, rolled the window down and before anyone said anything, I blurted out *"Don't worry mate you can try again in a month or so like your brother"* The instructor looked at me with disapproving eyes and said *"Do you have no faith in your son, he passed."*

Of course, I then tried to get Zac to drive round the block on his own, there is something very special or so I thought about that first time you go out on your own in a car but Zac point blank refused. We are pretty sure to this day that the examiner gave Zac a good talking to about being safe on the roads after he passed him and that has really made Zac very nervous and unwilling to drive on his own. He has driven once round the block, with a lot of bribery, I think it was the promise of take away for tea if he did it and he has driven once to McDonalds with Walt as a passenger for breakfast. After that though and probably because of Walt's commentary of the drive with emphasis on all of the things that Zac did wrong, like drive through Tesco car park the wrong way. We of course tried to point out that no one ever really drives the right way in a Tesco car park but that still didn't seem to matter or sink in. Zac only now, some 2 and a bit years later only seems to want to drive with Colin sitting next to him telling him what to do.

Walt passed on his second test and was very proud of himself. Although every time we have asked him to drive to work on his own or to hockey he has refused and said he didn't want to go or that he would walk instead. We worked out that if the route was something that had been done with Colin as part of their learning, I was always too nervous and panicky to sit with them in the car and still am, they would only drive there with Colin.

When Walt started university, he had every intention of driving to and from Buckingham rather than taking the X5. On his first day, we had prepared everything for him or so we thought. We had checked that he had got his car keys, house keys, that he knew where to park, we specified departure time, we programmed the Sat Nav and we filled the car up with fuel. We went off to work and I gave Walt strict instructions to call or text or me to tell me he had arrived safely. By 1pm there was nothing from him. I checked 'Find my iphone' only to see Walt was still at home. I called him:

"Er hi Walt, are you still at home?"

"Yes"

"Why? I thought you were gong to leave at 12pm to get there for 1pm"

"Well I would have done but I don't have a key."

"What do you mean you don't have a key?"

"I can't get in the car"

Oh my goodness, when it clicked I felt very silly; we had forgotten one simple item, the garage door key. Walt couldn't even get to the car because it was locked safely in the garage. I rushed home from work and managed to get him to his first tutorial just in time. After that experience, though Walt suggested that it would be a lot easier on the X5 and he could relax and study instead of having to think about the stress of driving. We of course agreed with this at this point.

We encouraged Walt last summer to take up a volunteer role at Bletchley Park so that he could see if being a historian would suit him. This gave us the opportunity to encourage him to drive himself. He had taken his test in Bletchley so it was familiar to him and armed with a Sat Nav and a Dashcam he found his way there with no problems at all. I of course tracked his every move on find my iPhone. When he returned he told us how other drivers were very silly, in particular one driver who just pulled out of the roundabout without looking. He described how he told him what for. Now as a parent, you do really worry about what they get up to and how they have coped with a situation so of course I went out and reviewed the Dashcam footage. The moment the other driver pulled out onto the roundabout straight in front of Walt, missing him by about 2 foot, there was a harsh braking sound followed by Walt announcing *"Oh dear"* and then driving calmly away. In my head I thought he have copied his Mother's behaviour in this type of situation and thrown in a few F's and Jeff's but no just a simple "Oh dear" sufficed for Walt.

Walt got a little more confident with his driving and decided that he would volunteer to take the polo team to training. Again I used my trusty 'Find my iPhone' or otherwise known now as 'Find my Walt' to track him. Me and Colin don't get invited out very often but this particular night we had been and I had suggested I would need to wait for Walt to return from his training session before heading out ourselves, just in case. We watched him drive up the M40, then down the M40, then back up the M40 and back down the M40, on the phone tracker. The worst thing about tracking them like this is there is nothing you can do to help as you watch them. When Walt eventually returned home I asked him what had happened. He simply said, *"the other people in the car had fallen asleep and I kept missing the turning off so the Sat Nav just kept turning me around."*

The last time, some 4 months ago, that Walt drove was when he decided to go to a University hockey training session, in the middle of nowhere. I had managed to get tickets to go to see Chris de Burgh with Colin and my Mum in Birmingham and had suggested that Walt should perhaps stay at home that evening just in case. Of course, he persuaded me that everything would be ok. As we were travelling up the M6 towards Birmingham, I tracked Walt on his journey. To my horror, he stopped for a very long time in the middle of nowhere; I was going to call him but remembered we had told him not use his phone while driving which of course he obeys. Then he started moving again but in the wrong direction and heading out towards goodness only knows where. I knew he had the Sat Nav on as we had programmed the hockey pitch location in for him but he was going totally the wrong way. After about 30 minutes he arrived home, so I called him.

"Walt it's Mum, what happened tonight"

"Well, you see I tried to go but then a fireman stopped me"

"Sorry what?"

"A fireman stopped me, in a yellow jacket and told me I had to turn round and that I didn't have my lights on and that was very dangerous, so I came home"

"But you put your lights on?"

"Yes the fireman helped me do that"

"Right and why did you have to turn round?"

"Big nasty accident"

"OK, so you are staying at home now then?"

"Yes"

Phew. Walt hasn't asked or wanted to drive again since this but we are pretty sure he will do soon. We are considering a bigger car for them both to drive with maybe an automatic gearbox. Of course this is not their choice it is totally mine. I think if I could I would give them a tank to drive but I am hoping a largish Volvo will keep them safe for now.

It's OK I am old enough

"It's OK I am old enough to look after the house now" was the first significant thing Zac said as we sped down the M1 towards Guildford at 9pm in late July 2019. An hour earlier I had received a call from Colin, who had been working away simply saying, *"I am in A&E"*. Then the phone went dead. This maybe explains the boys' telephone manner. I had no idea what part of the country my dearly beloved was. His work was taking him all over the world and I hate to admit it but all I started to know was what day he was leaving home and what day he would return, his actual whereabouts didn't really enter my head until that call.

After frantically trying to find his latest diary I worked out he would most likely be in the Royal Surrey County Hospital. I called the switchboard and asked to be put through to A&E. A very nice lady answered and explained that Colin had been taken into Resus and that she would get one of the consultants to call me. My first thought was car accident. The consultant rang me back and said Colin had been bought into Resus and that he was now stabilising but that they would need to keep him in overnight. He didn't explain what had happened but that I should maybe come down and make sure he had everything that he needed for an overnight stay.

I explained to the boys that Mum was going to drive to Guildford to make sure Dad was ok. Zac volunteered to come along for the ride and Walt suggested he would be best placed staying at home to look after the dogs. As we drove down the M1, Zac asked where dad was in the hospital and so I explained that he was in Resus so he must be in a pretty bad way. It was then that Zac turned to me and said the immortal words *"It's OK I am old enough to look after the house now"*. I reassured him that Dad was probably not going to leave us just yet, or I hoped that wouldn't be the case. The nearer we got to Guildford the nearer we got to signs pointing out places near beaches, Zac asked *"Mum when we have finished sorting Dad out can we go to the beach please?"* I declined of course explaining that it would be a bit late in the evening and that we should really get home to bed.

When we arrived at the hospital we noticed Colin's car parked in a space. I wandered over to it; a ticket had been neatly placed in the windscreen for the car park attendant it all felt very odd, how had Colin gone from obviously driving his car to being in Resus? It took me an age to work out how to use the ticket machine, it was one of those ones where you have to put all sorts of details in and it only accepted credit card payments, so how on earth had he managed all of that? We walked into the A&E Reception and I said who I was and whom I was there to see. The very nice lady said *"Ah yes, Mr Woolyur, he was in a terrible state when he came in, we took one look at him and rushed him straight down to Resus, I'll take you to him."*

We walked down a few corridors until we finally found the room with lots of machines that went ping and the recognisable face of my dearly beloved. There he was sitting in a hospital bed with wires and things all over him. I asked, *"What the dickens have you done?"* in a loving/caring kind of way. He explained that he had been eating at the local restaurant and a piece of meat they think had got lodged in his throat. As soon as Zac heard this he boldly marched up to Colin and said *"Dad what have I told you, you must always chew your food 10 times before swallowing!"* Of course Zac had never said this to Colin before, it was what Colin always says to them when they are bolting down one of their favourite meals.

Colin asked if we could go to his hotel and pick up his things and bring them back to him. We of course agreed. When we arrived at the hotel, Zac had a good look round the room and announced *"Dad has not got his money's worth from this room yet, I'm going to go and do a big poo in the toilet"* I would have laughed out loud but I was way too tired and just wanted to get back to Milton Keynes and go to bed. After I had of course, sorted Colin out for the night. Just as we were locking the hotel door up, Zac said *"We could stay here tonight mum then we could go to the beach tomorrow."* I declined much to his annoyance but suggested that we might have to get home to make sure Walt and the dogs were OK and that I had the small matter of work in the morning.

We sorted Colin out and then drove back to the hospital only to find Colin had been moved to a ward. Zac was not impressed, as this was not where we had left him. The journey home involved Zac keeping me awake with some very loud Power Metal. When we got home he said, *"That was fun but next time can we please go to the beach?"* I tried to explain that I hoped there wouldn't be a next time but if there was and we had time we might consider it just so we could go to bed.

Fortunately the next day when I received a call saying that a responsible adult needed to collect him because they had sedated him I called on my friend Sue to take me thus avoiding the need for any more beach related conversations.

Last words

If you remember from book one, Zac's first words were Octopus and Turtle. It's safe to say now some words are being strung together in sentences that make my eyes water. Zac has a form of Tourette's associated with his ASD. We first noticed a facial tic that Zac developed but looking back Zac has always liked to repeat random words. Only this week we watched some video's they had made on Photo Booth. Zac's consisted of saying over and over again "Big alligators mouth", "Count Dracula's teeth", "Mad Hatter's teeth" These were followed by some strange sounds like rip rip char and high pitched screams which we would liken and describe to others as the dying seagull.

We were told by the paediatrician not to be too concerned by the tics of the repeated phrases because it was all part of the autistic spectrum. Last Christmas, though I started to get a little concerned. We were driving back from an evening event when Zac announced *"Fucking Christmas lights."* At first I thought I had misheard him until it came again this time louder and with more force

"Fucking Christmas lights" so I said *"Pardon Zac?"*

He said, *"I didn't say anything"*

I was slightly confused and said *"are you sure?"*

"Yes" came the reply" We drove on and again *"Fucking Christmas lights"*.

"Zac, you keep saying, F'ing Christmas lights"

"Do I?"

"Yes"

And so it began. The next delightful set of phrases to appear was *"I'm going to fuck the dragon and its entire dragon family."* Now this is ok in the comfort of a bedroom away from people but what you don't want is it to be repeated over and over again in the local supermarket. Our response to it has been to mostly ignore it. Mainly because he doesn't know he is doing it but when it gets to the point that I think it's getting a bit too loud I will simply say *"Please don't make a dragon pregnant Zac I am not ready for grandchildren quite yet and especially not dragon ones"* He of course looks at me oddly and carries on with what he is doing. We are excited and somewhat nervous to see how this develops but we hope that we will fall back on a simple facial tic.

We are still concerned about the future and what comes after university, for Walt that could be December this year but what we will say is that both of our young gentlemen are amazing and they have so much to offer the world once you are trusted to be let in. And I should add if anyone knows a nice couple of girls out there please get in touch.

If you have enjoyed this book and haven't yet read Abbey's other two books:

Just Another Mum

And

Let the Teenage Years Begin

or buy both books combined in the
Monozygotic Chronicles

These are always available on Amazon and will go towards the ever-increasing retirement fund ☺

Printed in Great Britain
by Amazon